The Doomster's Monolithic Pocket Alphabet

THE DOOMSTER'S MONOLITHIC POCKET ALPHABET. First printing. November 2017. Published by Image Comics, Inc. Office of publication: 2701 NW Vaughn St., Suite 780, Portland, OR 97210. Copyright © 2017 Theo Prasidis & Maarten Donders. All rights reserved. "The Doomster's Monolithic Pocket Alphabet", its logos, and the likenesses of all characters herein are trademarks of Theo Prasidis & Maarten Donders, unless otherwise noted. "Image" and the Image Comics logos are registered trademarks of Image Comics, Inc. No part of this publication may be reproduced or transmitted, in any form or by any means (except for short excerpts for journalistic or review purposes), without the express written permission of Theo Prasidis & Maarten Donders, or Image Comics, Inc. All names, characters, events, and locales in this publication are entirely fictional. Any resemblance to actual persons (living or dead), events, or places, without satiric intent, is coincidental.

Printed in the USA.
For international rights, contact: foreignlicensing@imagecomics.com
ISBN: 978-1-5343-0595-3

IMAGE COMICS, INC. / Robert Kirkman: Chief Operating Officer / Erik Larsen: Chief Financial Officer / Todd McFarlane: President / Marc Silvestri: Chief Executive Officer / Jim Valentino: Vice President / Eric Stephenson: Publisher / Corey Murphy: Director of Sales / Jeff Boison: Director of Publishing Planning & Book Trade Sales / Chris Ross: Director of Digital Sales / Jeff Stang: Director of Specialty Sales / Kat Salazar: Director of PR & Marketing / Branwyn Bigglestone: Controller / Kali Dugan: Senior Accounting Manager / Sue Korpela: Accounting & HR Manager / Drew Gill: Art Director / Heather Doornink: Production Director / Leigh Thomas: Print Manager / Tricia Ramos: Traffic Manager / Briah Skelly: Publicist / Aly Hoffman: Events & Conventions Coordinator / Sasha Head: Sales & Marketing Production Designer / David Brothers: Branding Manager / Melissa Gifford: Content Manager / Drew Fitzgerald: Publicity Assistant / Vincent Kukua: Production Artist / Erika Schnatz: Production Artist / Ryan Brewer: Production Artist / Shanna Matuszak: Production Artist / Carey Hall: Production Artist / Esther Kim: Direct Market Sales Representative / Emilio Bautista: Digital Sales Representative / Leanna Caunter: Accounting Analyst / Chloe Ramos-Peterson: Library Market Sales Representative / Marla Eizik: Administrative Assistant / IMAGECOMICS.COM

The Doomster's Monolithic Pocket Alphabet

Words by **Theo Prasidis**
Illustrations by **Maarten Donders**

Prolegomenon

The year of our Lord 1970. Coldest February in ages. Friday the 13th. Under the pouring rain and rumbling thunder, an ominous knell. "Black Sabbath" is unleashed upon this mortal earth and the spacetime continuum is shifted beyond repair. This defining moment in human history gave birth to not only metal as we know it today, but to its gloomiest idiom as well, the heaviest form of music ever known to man, **DOOM**.

Almost five decades have passed since the initial shock. Doom metal has only grown stronger ever since, sowing its devil seed into dozens of other genres. It approached hard and progressive rock, it integrated extreme metal, it flirted with hardcore, it opened up to psychedelic culture, while always remaining true to its subterranean origins. Its founding fathers laid the groundwork, its second wave combatants secured the propagation, and its neophyte warlocks confirmed the inkling: doom is here to stay.

Over all these years, both doom artists and fans -doomsters from now on- have gradually developed their own rites, their own communicational codes, their own distinctive language. The book you're holding is a thorough exploration of a whole customary system, a result of painful research and unrestrained exposure to near-deafening decibels, presented in the surprising form of a colorfully illustrated alphabet.

A word of friendly warning, though. This is not your regular fancy picture book. Don't let its unparalleled cuteness delude you. This is the devil's work. Act accordingly.

To my little dude and budding doomster, Moisis

is for Amps

Instead of bricks, doomsters build their houses out of amps (preferably Orange Rockerverbs or Verellen Meatsmokes), in order to sustain a thick wall of sound.

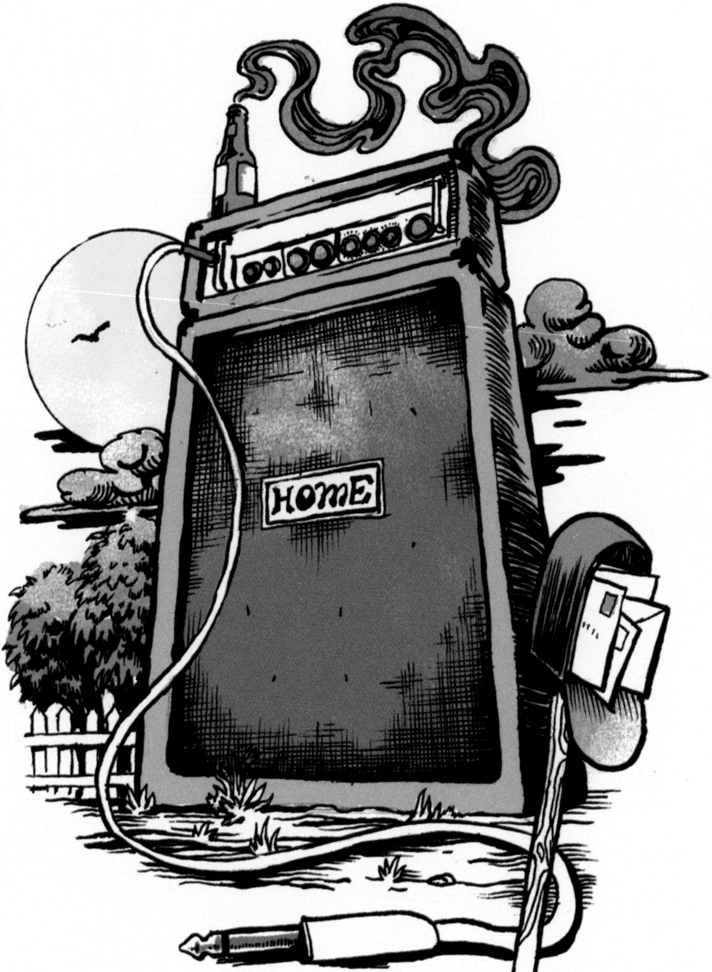
HOME

B

is for Bong

Graced by the blessings of the dark one, the bong is a certified ritualistic instrument used for mind alteration, shamanistic meditation and other western-friendly countercultural New Age marketing fads.

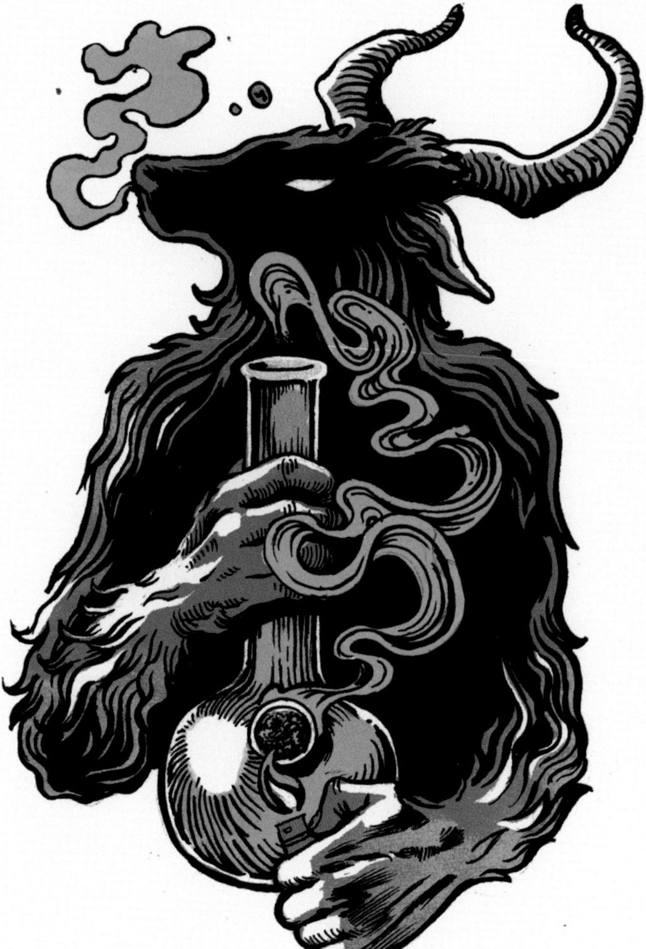

C

is for Churches

Despite their malicious ostentation, doomsters are not church burners. On the contrary, they appear to take a liking towards them, cathedrals in particular, and enjoy wearing crosses at times.

is for Druid

Ideally, a doomster's life is surrounded by magic herbs. Hence, every doomster's wet dream is to become a druid. Or meet one. Or at least write a song about one.

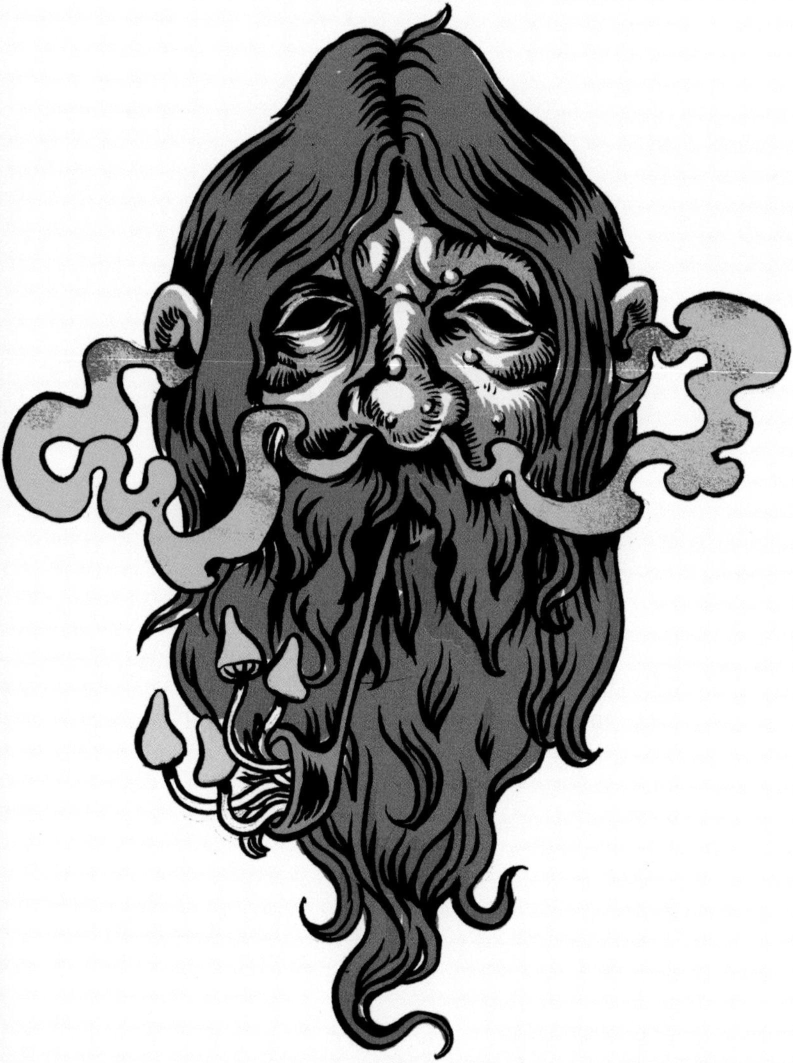

is for Epic

From the godly collisions of *Gilgamesh*, to the vast seas of the *Odyssey*, to the hellish pyres of the *Divine Comedy*, to the holy light of *Nightfall*, epic poetry has come a long way.

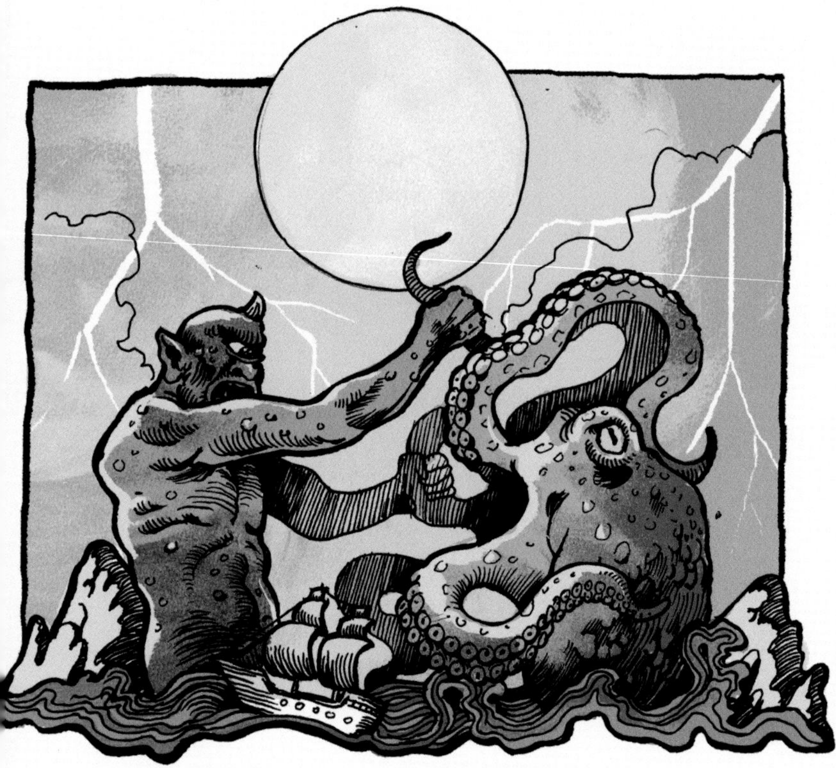

is for Flares

Black leather and combat boots are so hopelessly nineties. Modern-day doomsters, similar to proto-doomsters, wear flares.

Deal with it.

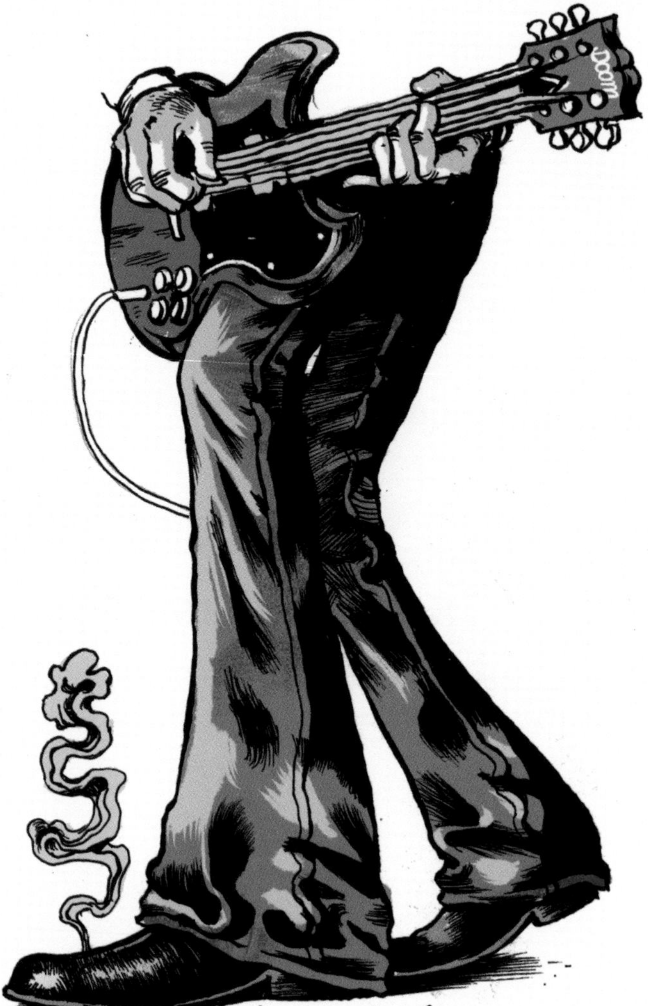
Doom

is for Goats

Goats are 100% Satan-approved pets for doomsters, along with crows, sloths and extremely grumpy black cats.

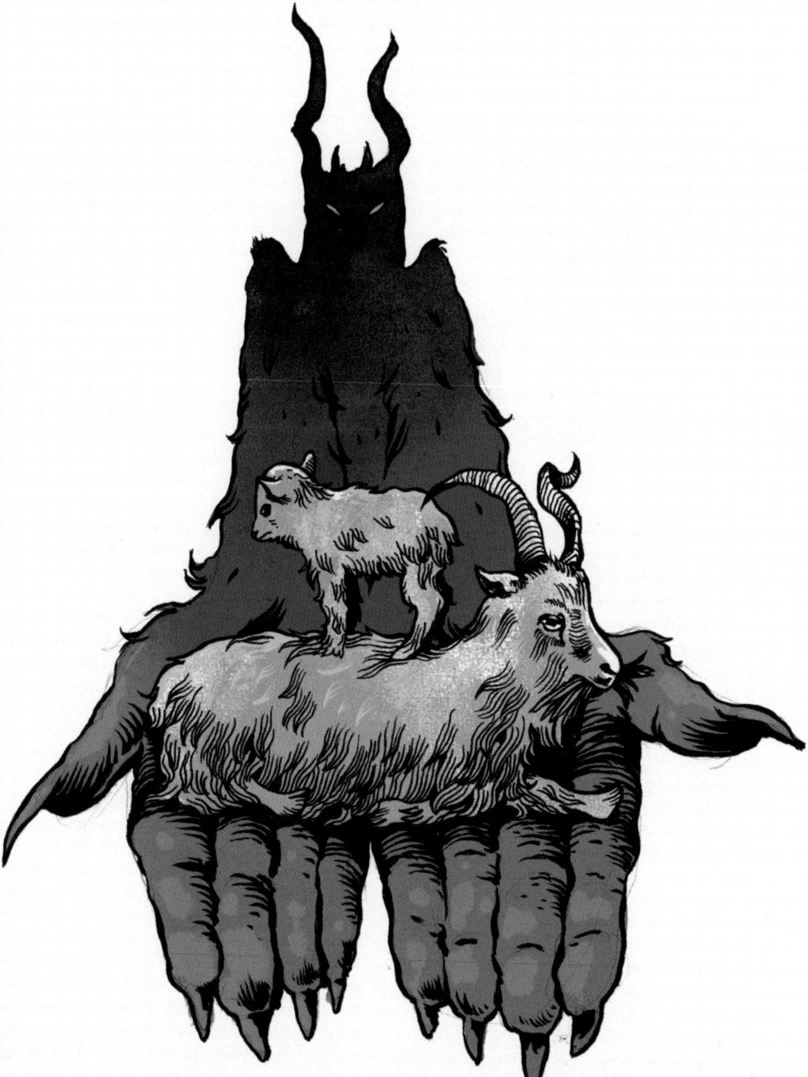

is for Hammer

Doomsters are acquainted with the entire Hammer Films back catalogue from the mid-1950s to the early 1970s. Additionally, they know every Christopher Lee, Peter Cushing and Vincent Price quote by heart and fantasize about Caroline Munro's bosom on a daily basis.

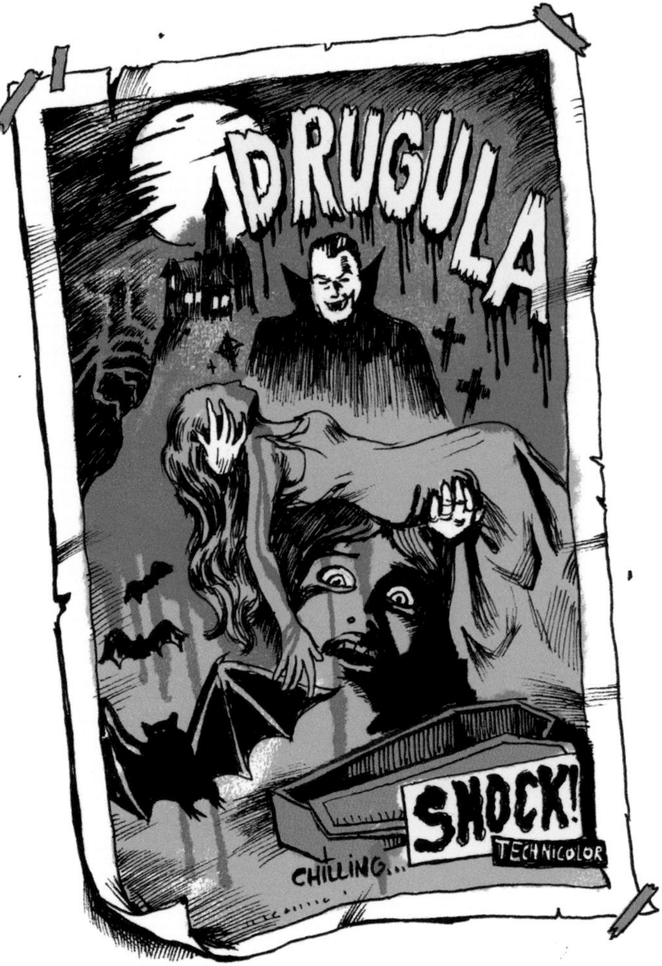
DRUGULA
SHOCK!
TECHNICOLOR
CHILLING...

is for Iommi

"Praise Iommi, for Iommi is good; Sing praises to His name, for it is lovely."

The Bible Black, Psalm 135:666

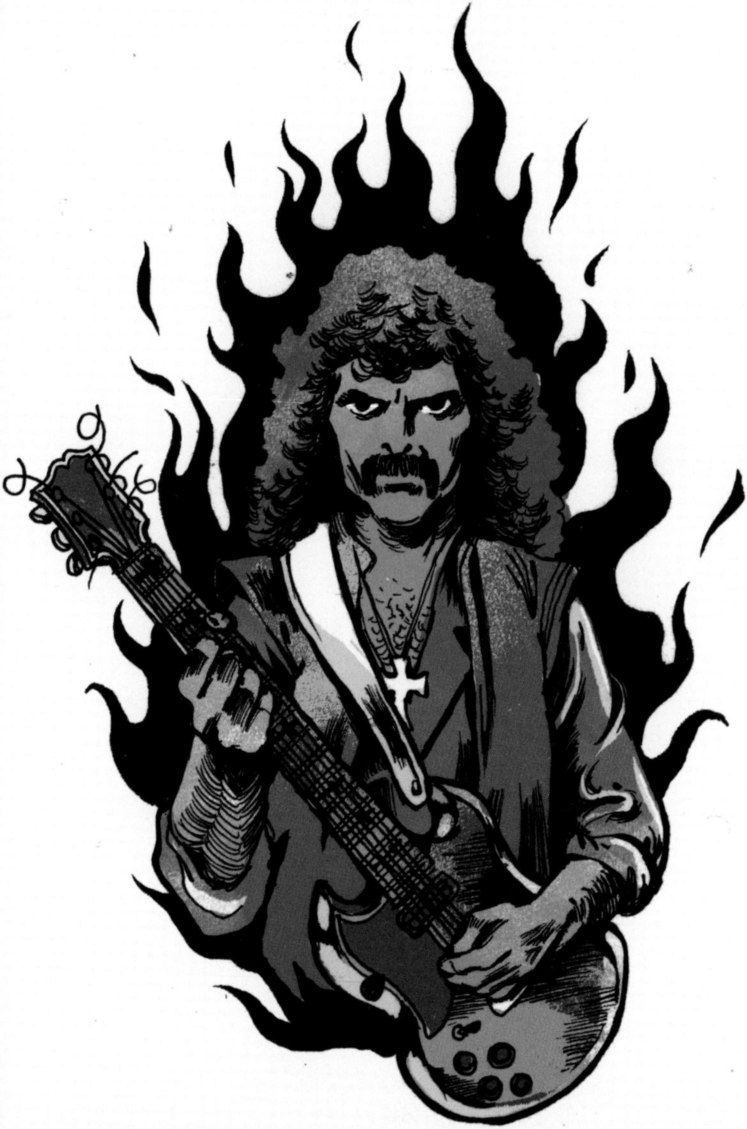

J

is for JJ Koczan

Upon the gates of doom-heaven brace thyself, for thou shalt be judged by the genre's own St. Peter, JJ Koczan, aka The Obelisk, aka HP Taskmaster, aka The Man. Pray for a positive critique. Or be eternally doomed.

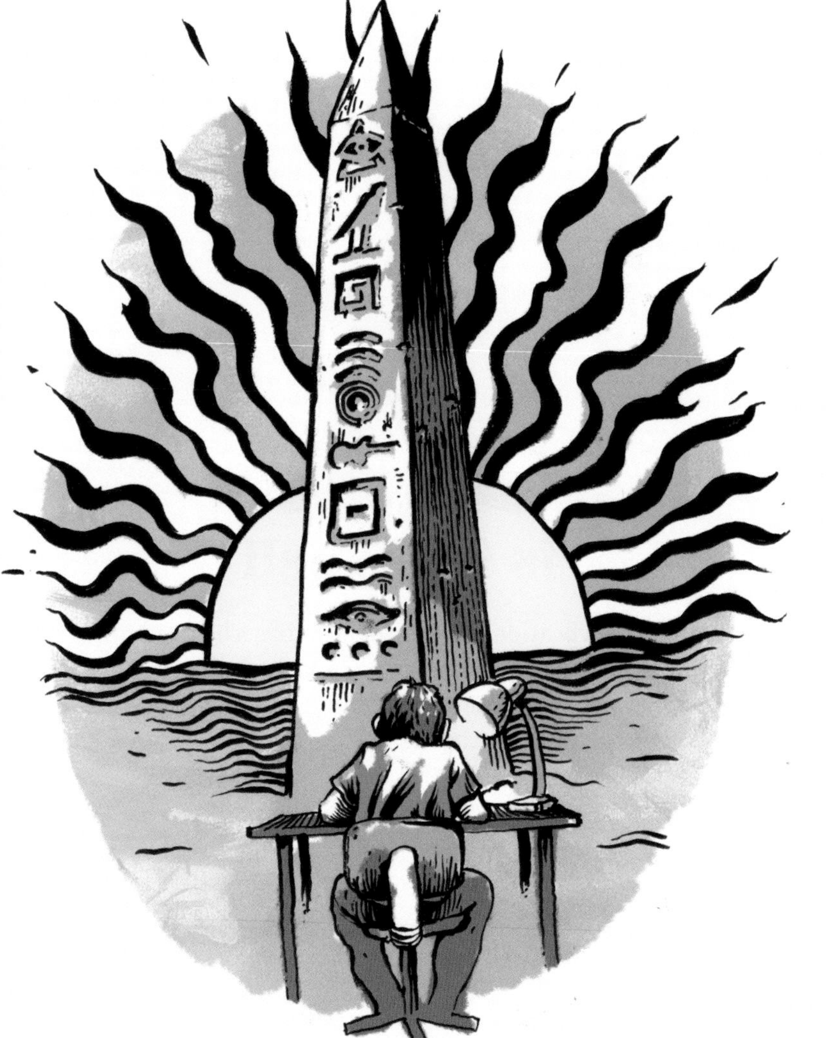

is for Knell

The ancestral vocation. The primal rumble. The fundamental noise. The definitive call to doom. Upon sounding, doomsters customarily suspend all activity, execute the wide power stance and throw up the horns.

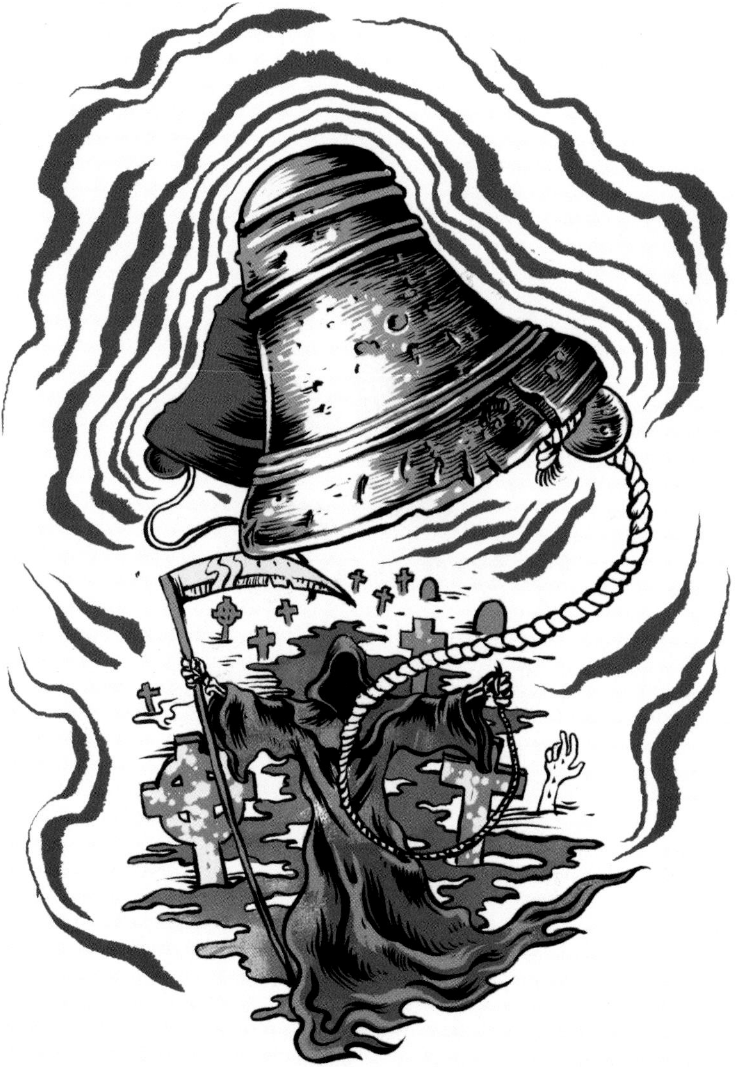

L
is for Lovecraft

Doomsters deeply admire the works of the master of unspoken cosmic horrors and unabashed xenophobic notions, H.P. Lovecraft. Furthermore, since everything he has written falls into the public domain, they are allowed to rip him off without being bothered.

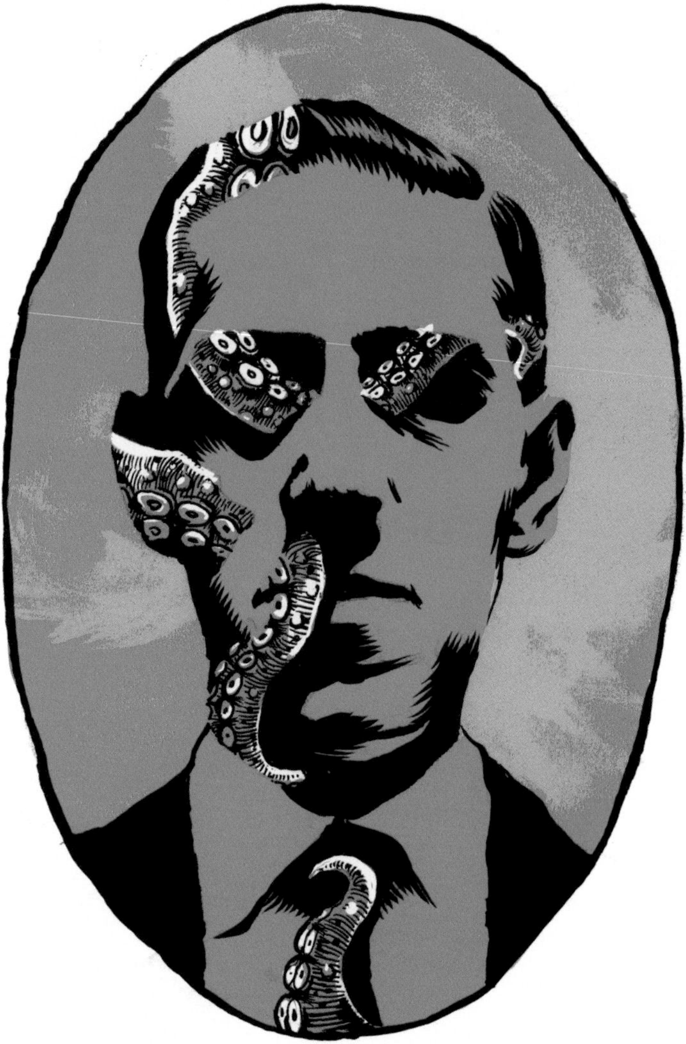

is for Mistress

She stands before you. A figure in black which points at you. She goes by many names: Johanna, Dorthia, Jennie-Ann, Alia, Tania, Rebecca, Lori, Uta, Ozma, Jess, Jex, Jinx.

She is not a Disney Princess. She is the Doom Mistress. And she's coming to get you.

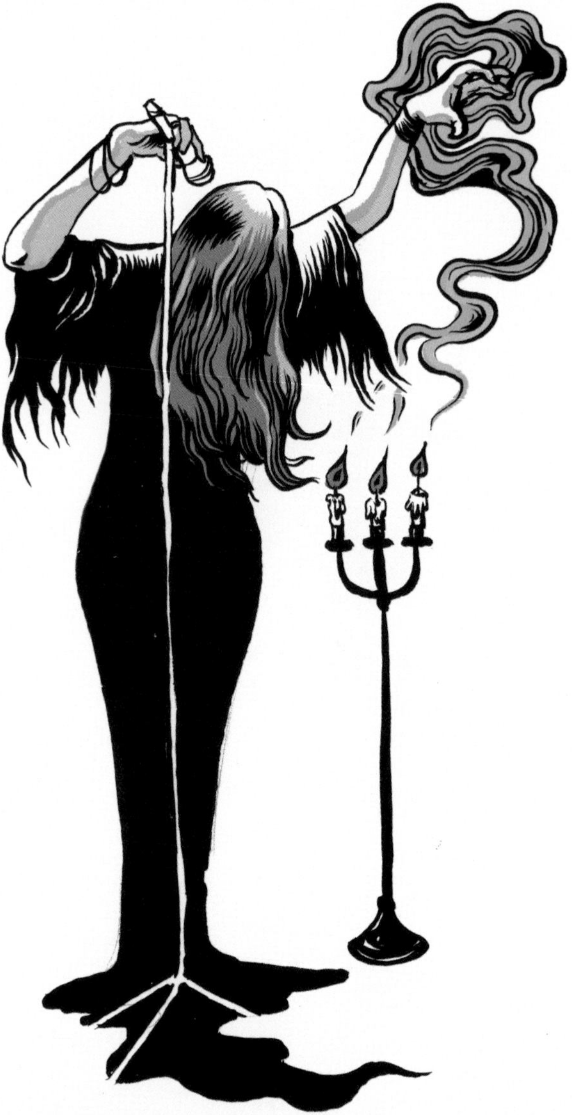

is for Nuns

Mostly naked ones.

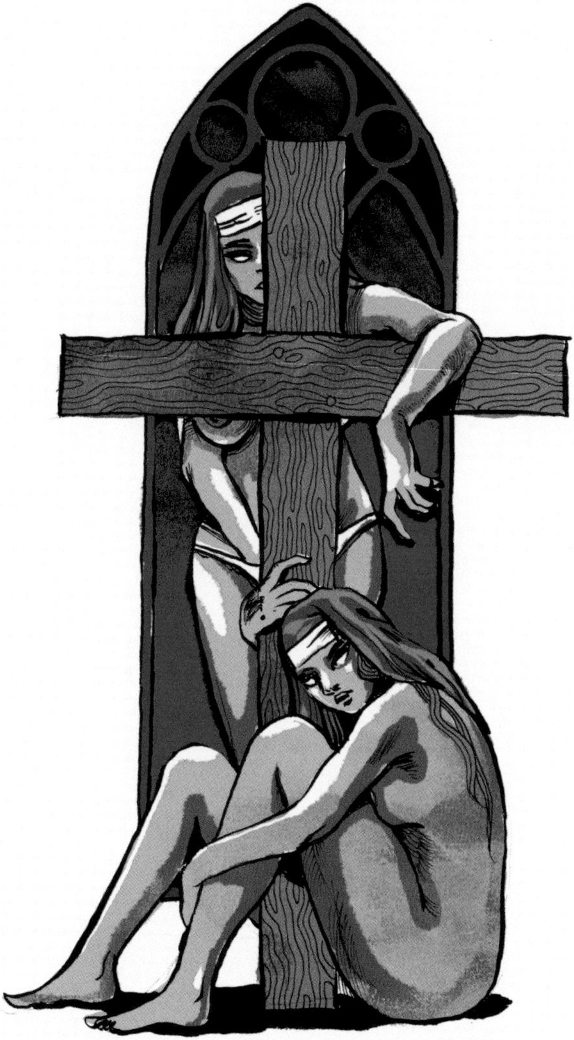

O

is for Occult

Doomsters are drawn to the occult like mosquitoes are drawn to UV lights. Provide them with pretty much anything of unearthly, arcane, paranormal, mystical, magical, alchemical, cabalistic, obscure, hidden, psychic or weird nature, and they're game.

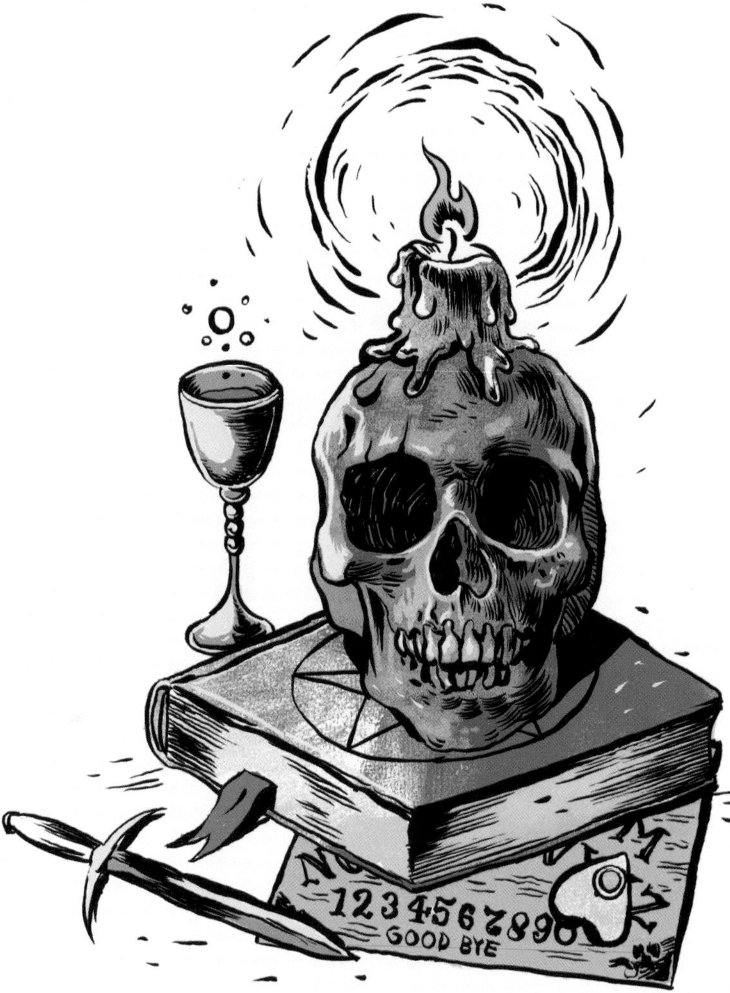

1234567890
GOOD BYE

P

is for Purple

Every doomster's favorite color and an obligatory inclusion in all true doom metal cover artworks. It effectively evokes dreadful visions of vertiginous bewilderment, supernatural wonderment and Prince.

Q

is for Quantum Mystic

Doomsters occupy themselves with the study of Quantum Physics, largely focusing on electrodynamics, curved spacetime and the hypothesis of the Hawkwind Radiation, predicted to be emitted by candle-massive black holes.

After exhaustive penetration and psychosomatic devotion to the field, they become eligible to receive the chrism of the Quantum Mystic by the spiritual leader of the Yob cult, Mike Scheidt.

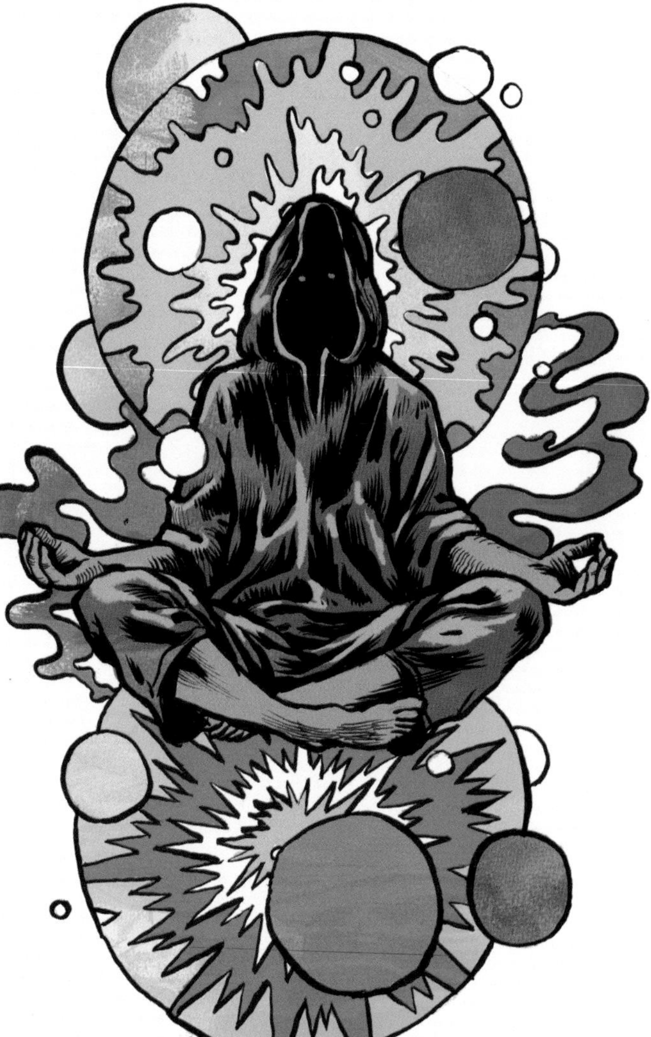

is for Riff

The only true religion. To reach divinity, doomsters are said to follow the smoke toward the riff-filled land.

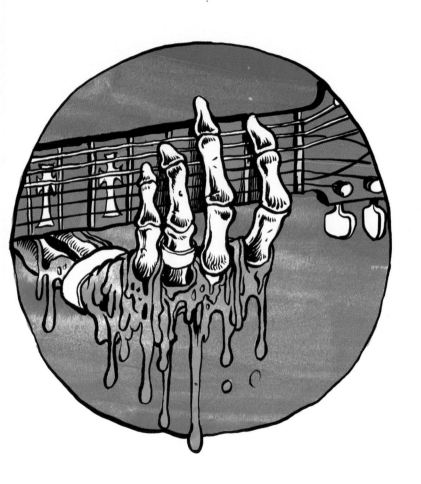

S

is for Shroomies

Amanita, Galerina, Pholiotina, Gymnopilus, Boletus, Pluteus, Panaeolus, Copelandia, Mycena, Panaeolina, Conocybe, Inocybe, Psilocybe. Whatever floats your goat, man.

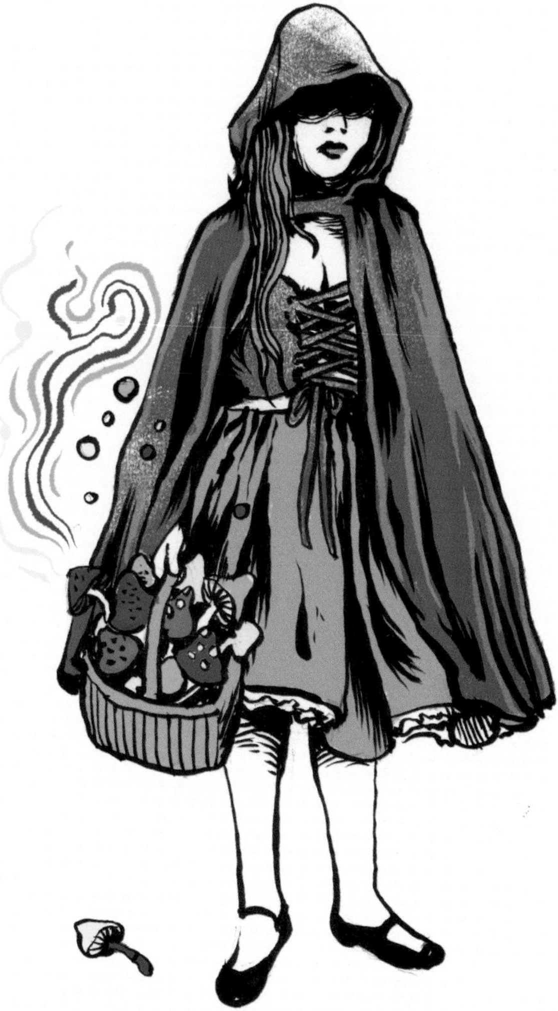

is for Tempo

Doomsters like their tempo how they like their orgasms: slow.

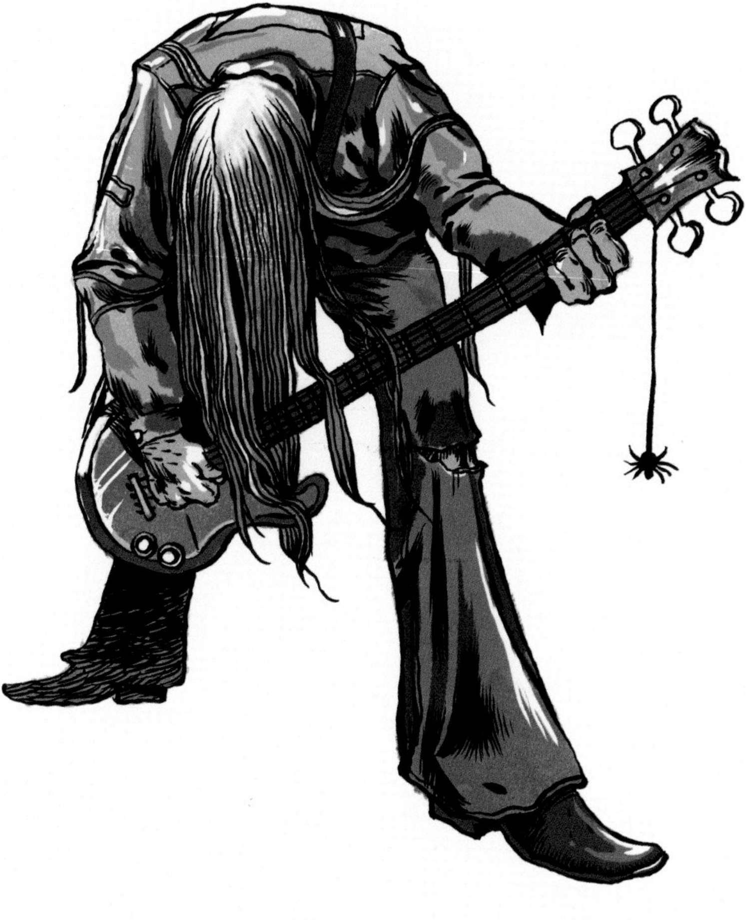

is for UK

Land of the tea. Home of the grave. Mecca of doom.

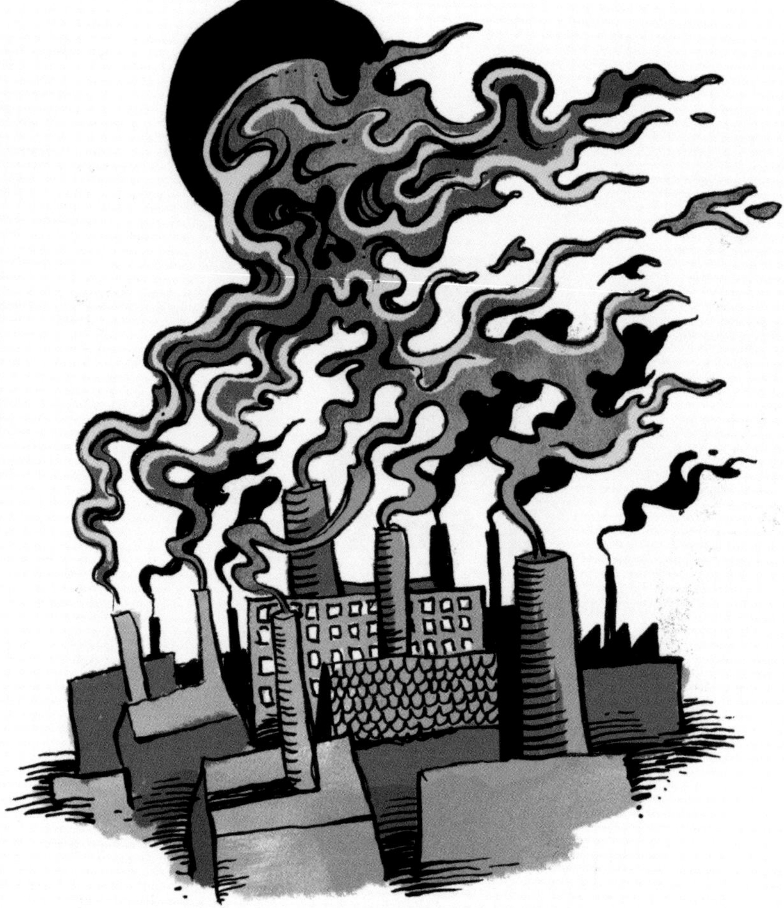

is for Vinyl

The only acceptable format to appreciate the value of a true doom metal album. If it's been produced into more than 500 copies, its trueness is highly questionable.

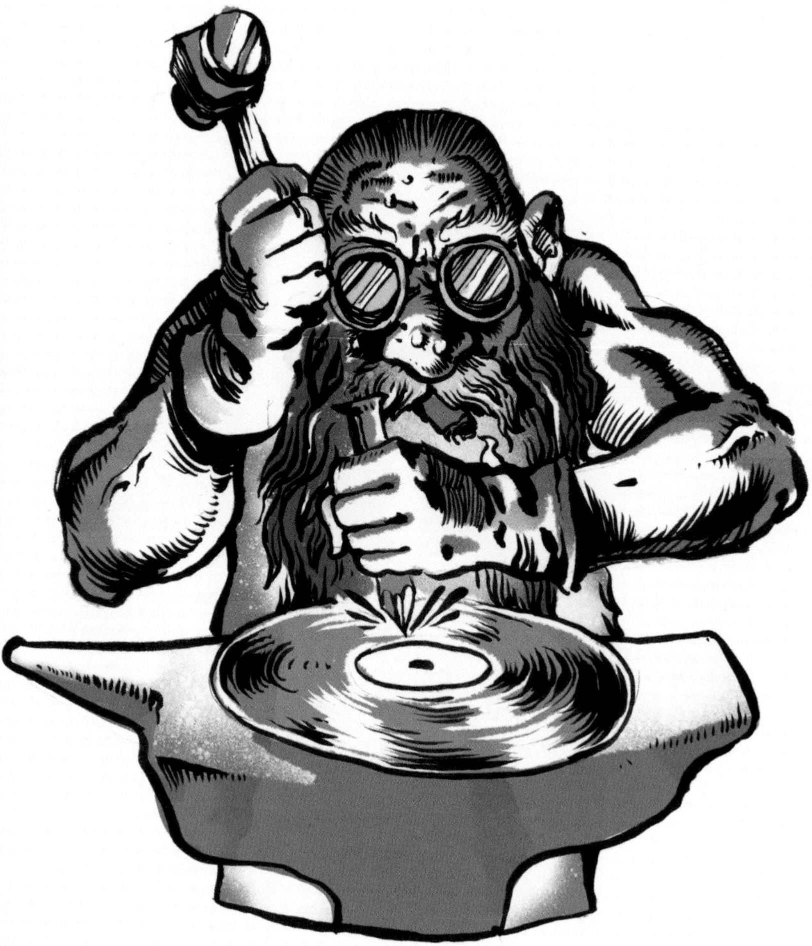

is for Weedian

If Baphomet is the lord of doom, then Weedian is his prophet. Now an action figure. Weed sold separately.

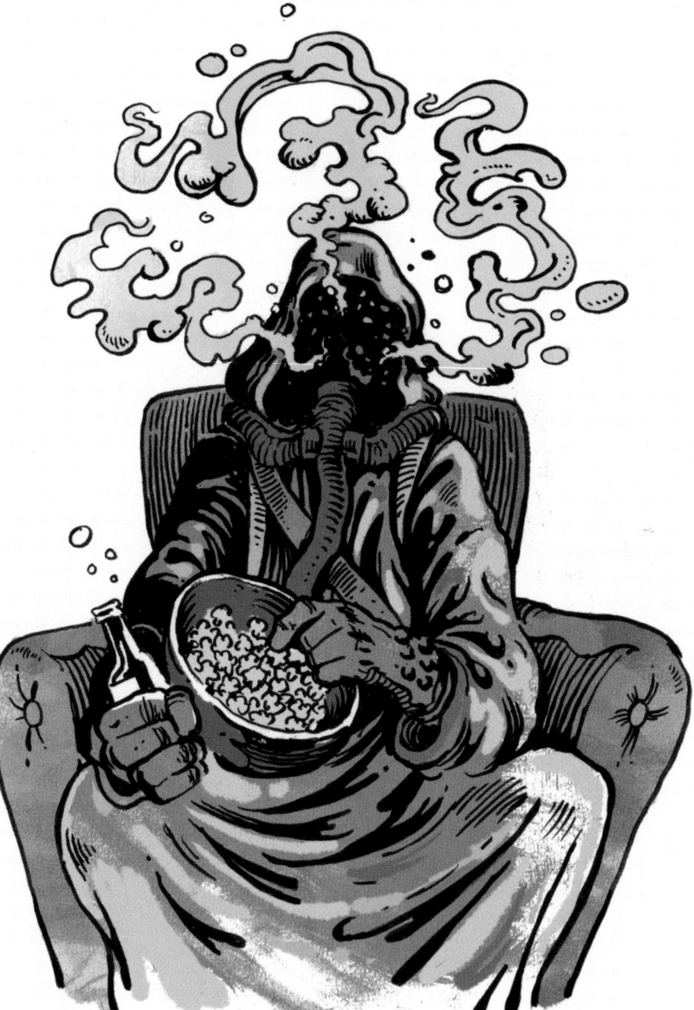

is for Xanax

Anywhere up to 6 mg per day, for the love of Sleep.

Y

is for Yoga

There is such a thing as Doom Yoga. When doomsters take a break from pain, misery and desperation, they're balancing their Yin and Yang practicing vinyasa-based yoga. Class repertoire covers everything from the claustrophobic drones of Sunn O))), Nadja and early Earth, to the traditional pentatonic grooves of Black Sabbath, Pentagram and Saint Vitus.

More like, Zen Vitus.

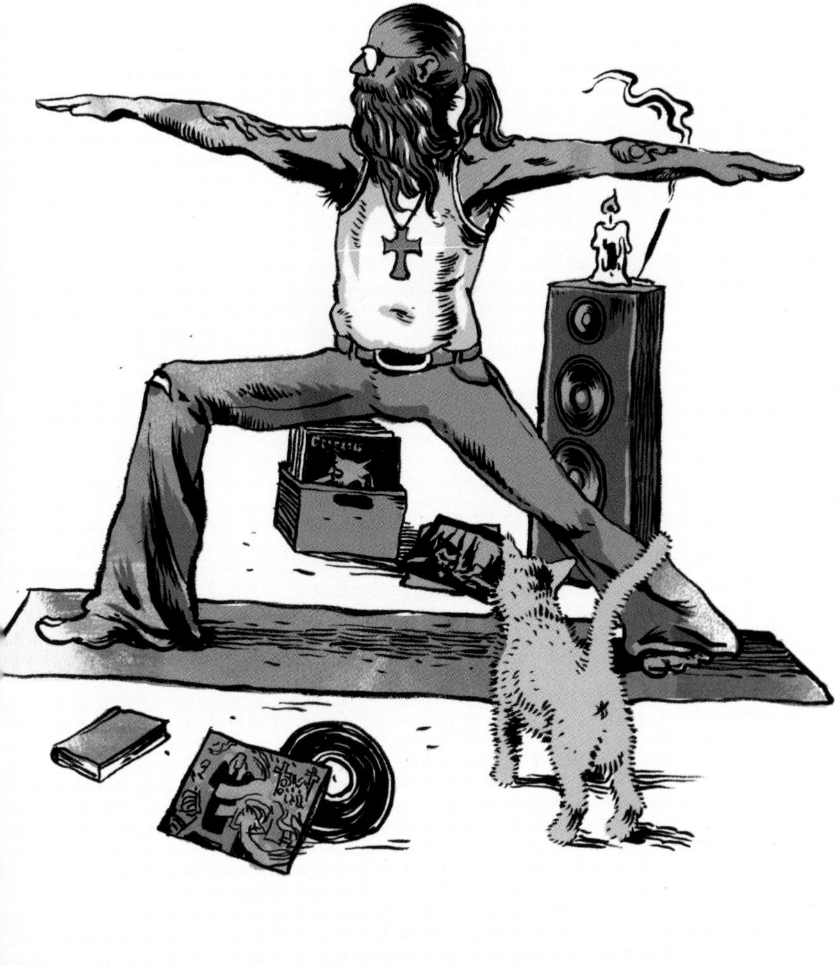

Z

is for Zoning

While normal people are zoning for a few seconds, or minutes at most, doomsters' zones can last many hours, days even. Legend tells of a doomster who died of deep zoning, while listening to the endless groove on Side A of Cathedral's *Forest Of Equilibrium* for one hundred and forty-seven days. Some say the neighbours can still hear the vinyl spinning.

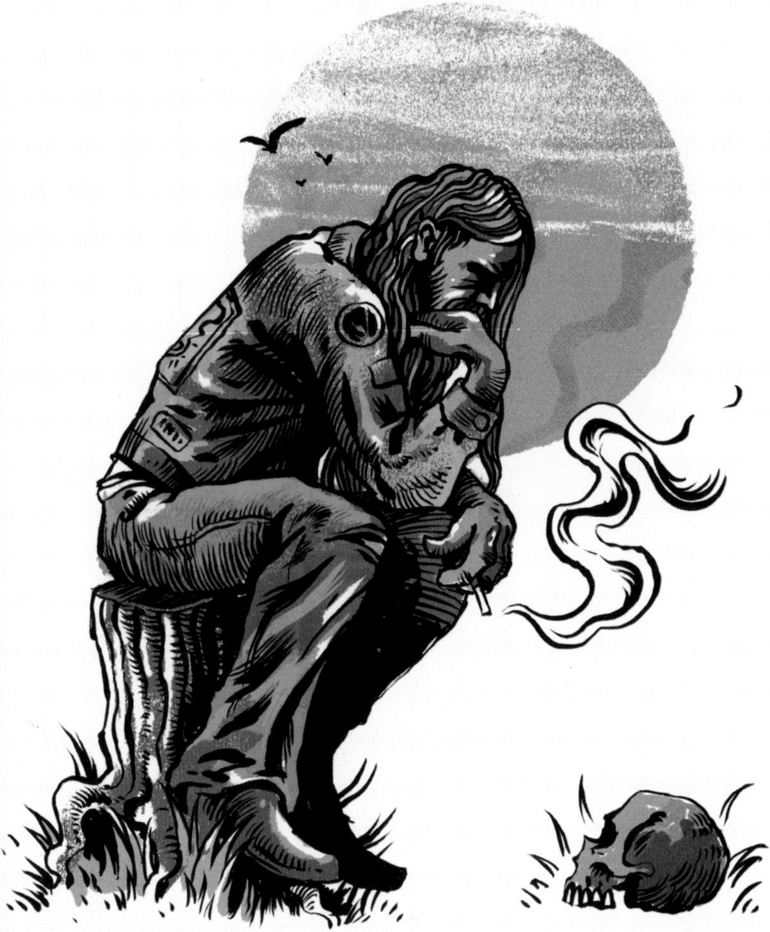

About the Author

Champion of the obscure Cult Film and Television master's degree from Ye Olde London's Brunel University, Theo is a full-on cult media sucker, a manic consumer of any visual or auditory expression of pulpness, occultism, nostalgia and psychedelia. He has occasionally earned some money as a festival curator, an event coordinator, a film critic and columnist, a social media manager, a graphic designer, a commercial photographer, a DJ, a barman and a house cleaner. His latest antics include the launching of an indie record label and the uninvited intrusion into the world of comics.

About the Illustrator

After graduating as illustrator from the St. Joost art academy (Breda, NL) in 2008, Maarten has independently provided handmade illustrations, logos, designs and creative direction for musicians, bands, record labels, magazines, breweries, music venues and the likes. Being an avid concert-goer and record collector, he always had a clear goal to combine his art with his passion for music. His work has graced album covers, posters, clothing, beer bottles etc. Maarten occasionally exhibits his work, and since 2009 he has regularly contributed art to the legendary Roadburn Festival in Tilburg.

Maarten's primary focus as an illustrator is on personality and authenticity. He uses his sketchbook and personal interests as a launching point, where every idea is equally important, and anything can ignite a spark. His goal: to create powerful, expressive images that are recognizable, unique and breathe personality.

Weedian character created by Arik Moonhawk Roper for the cover art of Sleep's *Dopesmoker* 2012 reissue via Southern Lord Records

Cathedral's *Forest of Equilibrium* was released on December 1991 via Earache Records

Acknowledgements to Eliana & Alexandra, Walter Hoeijmakers, Mike Scheidt, Arik Roper, JJ Koczan, Stef Dimou, Green Yeti, Yannis Efthymiou, Aris Labos, Melandros Ganas, Kostas Zachopoulos, Piotr Wyrosław Dobry.

DOOM OR BE DOOMED